Renovate a RIVER

By William Anthony

Minneapolis, Minnesota

Credits

Cover – BMJ, MarySan, Bika Ambon, Kevin Wells Photography, faqeeh, My Good Images. 4–5 – VarnaK, Frithjof Moehle. 6–7 – Erol Savci, blazg. 8–9 – Denis Belitsky, RITSU MIYAMOTO, Milos Dumic. 10–11 – Fedorov Oleksiy, Janusz Lipinski, Creative Stall. 12–13 – mahey, Miks Mihails Ignats. 14–15 – MaryDesy, Kolonko, gvictoria, worldclassphoto, y.s.graphicart. 16–17 – Amanita Silvicora, Maquiladora, PRILL, Kletr, Nadya_Art, A7880S. 18–19 – Rock and Wasp, Dmitry Rukhlenko, Seahorse Vector, faqeeh, VectorShow. 20–21 – Travel mania, Aun Photographer, freshcare, Mark_Rimsky, Aleksandar Malivuk. 22–23 – Victoria Lisak, Tatyana Okhitina, Far700, Svitlana Tytska, Marina Akinina.

Library of Congress Cataloging-in-Publication Data is available at www.loc.gov or upon request from the publisher.

ISBN: 978-1-63691-923-2 (hardcover)
ISBN: 978-1-63691-929-4 (paperback)
ISBN: 978-1-63691-935-5 (ebook)

© 2023 Booklife Publishing
This edition is published by arrangement with Booklife Publishing.

North American adaptations © 2023 Bearport Publishing Company. All rights reserved. No part of this publication may be reproduced in whole or in part, stored in any retrieval system, or transmitted in any form or by any means, electronic, mechanical, photocopying, recording, or otherwise, without written permission from the publisher.

For more information, write to Bearport Publishing, 5357 Penn Avenue South, Minneapolis, MN 55419. Printed in the United States of America.

Contents

How to Build Our World 4

Find the Source 6

Build the Upper Course 8

Make the Middle Course 10

Finish the River 12

Place the Plants 14

Add the Animals 16

Bring In Some Boats 18

Put In a Port 20

Make Your Own Environment . . . 22

Glossary 24

Index 24

How to Build Our World

Our world is amazing. It is full of places to go and things to see. There are different **environments**, from deserts to rivers. Each one has plants, animals, and more.

What does a river environment look like? Let's build one to find out!

Find the Source

A river is a long **body** of water that **flows** from one place to another. The place where the water starts is called the source. Let's find a source for our river!

A river's source could be a lake. Or it could be another river. The source could even be an underground pool of water.

Many rivers start on hills or mountains.

Rivers flow downhill from their sources.

Build the Upper Course

Now that we've found a source, we can start building our river. Rivers have three main parts called courses. The source flows into the upper course.

The land near a river's upper course may be **steep** with lots of **valleys**.

Make the Middle Course

Next, we'll build a middle course for our river.
The upper course flows into the middle course.

The middle course of a river is wider and deeper than the upper course.

The middle course has big curves called bends. River bends are shaped when fast-moving water cuts through land.

A river's water usually flows fastest in the middle course.

11

Finish the River

We're almost done building our river. We just need to add the lower course and the mouth.

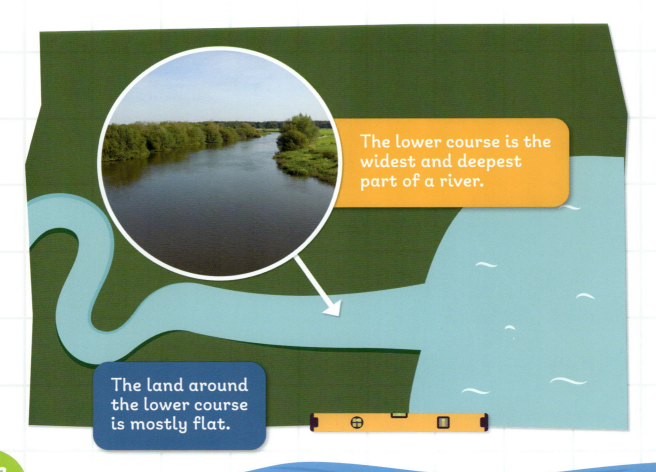

The lower course is the widest and deepest part of a river.

The land around the lower course is mostly flat.

A river ends by dumping its water into a lake or ocean. This part of the river is called the mouth.

13

Sometimes, river water goes onto nearby land. The water soaks into the **soil** and helps plants grow.

The soil near a river mouth is very **fertile**. This means it is great for growing plants.

Add the Animals

Next, we'll add animals to our river. Some river animals live only in water. Others live only on land. And some animals can do both.

Hippos live on land near rivers. But they often sit in the water, too!

Many kinds of fish live in rivers.

Rivers in different places around the world have different animals.

Bring In Some Boats

People can also spend time on our river.
Let's hop in a boat and see where we can go . . .

People may take boats on rivers to get from one place to another.

Some people use small boats called kayaks for fun.

There are people who live on rivers all the time! They stay on special boats called houseboats.

Put In a Port

Let's build one more thing to help people use our river. We'll add a port!

A port is a place where ships can drop off or pick up people and goods.

Goods are things that people need or want. Goods can be anything from food to toys.

Many ships travel across oceans. They may stop at ports.

21

Make Your Own Environment

River environments are incredible! They can have wonderful waterfalls, pretty plants, and awesome animals. Now, it's time to build your own environment! You could draw it, paint it, or write about it. What do you want to put in your river?

What will be the source of your river?

How will people use your river?

Which animals will live by your river?

23

Glossary

body a whole area of something

environments the different parts of our world in which people, animals, and plants live

fertile able to help plants grow

flows moves in a smooth, steady stream

rapids parts of a river where the water flows quickly over steep land or rocks

shallow having little space between the top and bottom of something

soil dirt that plants grow in

steep having a sharp slope

valleys areas of low land between mountains or hills

Index

lakes 6, 13
mountains 7
mouths 12–13, 15, 21
oceans 13, 21
people 18–21, 23
rapids 9
soil 15
valleys 8
waterfalls 9, 22